Wildcat Run

Sonya
Spreen Bates

Illustrated by
Kasia Charko

ORCA BOOK PUBLISHERS

Library and Archives Canada Cataloguing in Publication

Bates, Sonya Spreen
Wildcat run / Sonya Spreen Bates ; illustrated by Kasia Charko.
(Orca echoes)

Issued also in electronic format.
ISBN 978-1-55469-830-1

I. Charko, Kasia, 1949- II. Title. III. Series: Orca echoes
PS8603.A8486W54 2011   JC813'.6   C2011-903505-7

First published in the United States, 2011
Library of Congress Control Number: 2011907477

Summary: When Lexie wipes out on the ski slope, Jake and Tommy have to find a way
to get help while a cougar prowls in the nearby woods.

Orca Book Publishers gratefully acknowledges the support for its publishing programs
provided by the following agencies: the Government of Canada through the Canada Book
Fund and the Canada Council for the Arts, and the Province of British Columbia
through the BC Arts Council and the Book Publishing Tax Credit.

*Orca Book Publishers is dedicated to preserving the environment and has printed this book
on paper certified by the Forest Stewardship Council®.*

Cover artwork and interior illustrations by Kasia Charko

ORCA BOOK PUBLISHERS
PO Box 5626, Stn. B
Victoria, BC Canada
V8R 6S4

ORCA BOOK PUBLISHERS
PO Box 468
Custer, WA USA
98240-0468

www.orcabook.com
Printed and bound in Canada.

14 13 12 11 • 4 3 2 1

For Eric,
who had his own adventure in the snow.

Chapter One
ON THE SLOPES

Jake adjusted his ski goggles. He pulled his gloves firmly onto his hands.

I am a ski patrol, he thought, *on my way to a rescue at the top of the mountain.*

Jake's cousin, Lexie, zipped up her down jacket. The line moved forward. They shuffled closer to the chairlift, pulling Jake's brother, Tommy, along with them.

Jake was excited. They had been at Mount Whitmore all week, and it was the first time they were going up the hill on their own. He still couldn't believe Dad had agreed. When Dad twisted his knee on the last run, Jake thought they would have to go back to the lodge early. But with an hour of daylight left, Dad had reluctantly told them they could go for another run on their own.

"Make sure you take Easy Street or Gentle Giant," he said. "Stick together and look after Tommy. You know he can't go as fast as you and Lexie."

Jake and Lexie had promised to be careful, and they had all rushed off for the lift.

I have my rescue crew with me and my emergency pack on my back, thought Jake. Dad always carried an emergency first-aid kit. He had insisted Jake take it with them. *The skiers wait for help, scared and cold. It grows dark.*

Jake looked up to where the clouds covered the sun. It *was* getting dark. It got dark early in the mountains. And it looked like it might snow. This would probably be their last trip up the lift.

They moved to the front of the line. Jake sidestepped into position as the chairlift looped around on its track.

Tommy slipped on an icy patch, and Jake grabbed onto his arm so he wouldn't fall. The chair scooped them up. Lexie pulled the bar down over their laps.

Legs swinging, Jake looked back at the line of skiers waiting for the lift. Dad waved. Jake gave him a thumbs-up and glanced over at his brother, Tommy, puffed up like a snowman in a dark green snowsuit. Tommy was hopeless. Even though he had skied heaps of times, he still snowplowed down the easy runs. He was slower than a turtle on snowshoes. Tommy was always ruining things for Jake. If it wasn't for Tommy, they could go down one of the harder runs, like Pine Valley or Black Bear Creek or maybe Wildcat Run. Lexie said Wildcat Run was the best run on the slopes. It wasn't the steepest or the fastest, but it wound around the back side of Mount Whitmore and had some wicked drops.

"So, are we going for Easy Street again?" said Lexie. "Or should we try something really crazy like Lollipop Lane?"

and forth, sending a spray of snow shooting off his skis with each turn. Faster and faster he went. It was hard to slow down. Lexie had stopped to wait for him, but he whipped past her, unable to stop. His skis rattled over an icy patch, and he almost fell. His heart thumped. Up ahead the track rounded a bend. He pointed his skis together in a snow-plow. If he didn't slow down, he would never make the corner.

The snow sprayed over the front of his skis. He leaned into them and felt himself slowing. It was just enough. He flew through the bend. His stomach dropped as he hit a hidden dip, and his skis left the ground. Then he landed, throwing his arms around to keep his balance. The hill leveled out, and he slid to a stop.

Bending over to catch his breath, he didn't know whether to laugh or cry.

Lexie slid to a stop beside him, spraying him with snow. "What happened to taking it slow?" she said with a grin.

Jake shook his head. "That was awesome," he said.

"I told you," said Lexie.

Then they heard a scream.

"Tommy," they said together.

Chapter Three
TRACKS

Tommy rounded the bend, his skis were pointed together in a snowplow, and his arms stuck straight out like a scarecrow's. His face looked like a comic-book character. His eyes were bugged out, and his mouth was shaped in an *O*. He bumped through the dip, whirled his arms around like a windmill and fell.

Jake started up the hill toward him.

"I'm all right," said Tommy, sitting up. One of his skis had come off, and the other one stuck out sideways at an awkward angle. Jake snapped the clasp open, and Tommy struggled to his feet. His boots sank into the soft snow at the edge of the run.

"Did you see how fast I was going?" Tommy asked Jake, his eyes shining.

"Yeah, you were going fast all right," Jake said. He winked at Lexie. He thought Tommy had been going pretty slow, compared to him.

"You were racing," said Lexie.

Tommy beamed.

Jake looked around for Tommy's other ski. He spotted it in the trees not far away. "There's your ski. I'll get it," he said.

Jake slid down the little slope and snowplowed to a stop. Reaching down to pick up the ski, something caught his eye. All around him the snow was smooth, untouched except for the tracks his skis had just made. But on the other side of the tree was a set of prints that sent a chill up his spine. Paw prints. And they were big. As big as Jake's hand.

"Come on, Jake," called Lexie. "We haven't got all night."

Jake stared at the prints. Could they really be what he thought they were?

"Hey, Lexie, come down here," he said. He gestured urgently and peered into the trees.

Lexie skied down to Jake. Putting a finger to his lips, Jake pointed toward the tracks.

Lexie gasped. "Cat tracks," she said. She bent to look at the prints. "They're big. Probably a cougar." She touched one with her finger, leaving a small indent in the snow. "And they're fresh too." She squinted up the hill, in the direction the prints headed. "Cougars are most active at dusk. We better get back to the lodge."

"How do you know so much about cougars?" asked Jake.

"I told you. The Internet," said Lexie. "Let's go."

Jake grabbed Tommy's ski and shuffled back up the slope to where Tommy was waiting.

"What's down there?" asked Tommy. "Can I see?"

"No, it's nothing," said Jake. "Let's get going. I bet Mom will make us hot chocolate when we get back."

"Yum!" said Tommy.

Jake's stomach was all knotted up as they headed down the hill. He didn't know much about cougars, but he knew they were big. Big enough to kill a sheep on his grandparents' farm a few years back.

They skied in single file with Lexie in the lead. Tommy followed and Jake brought up the rear. Lexie took it slow, looking back to make sure Tommy was keeping up.

They had skied for only a minute or two when Jake heard something in the trees. It sounded like branches snapping. Lexie must have heard it too. She signaled for them to stop, and Jake and Tommy pulled up beside her. They heard the crack of a twig and the thump of snow falling off a tree branch.

Chapter Four
RACE FOR YOUR LIFE

"What's that in the bushes?" Tommy whispered.

No one answered. Then something exploded out of the trees behind them. A deer bounded across the ski run and disappeared into the forest.

A snarl split the air, and a huge golden cat streaked across the snow. It raced after the deer.

"Jake!" screeched Tommy. "There's a—"

Jake clamped a hand over Tommy's mouth. "Let's go!" Jake said.

Lexie and Tommy took off, and Jake sped after them. A cougar. Here on Wildcat Run. And only meters away from them!

Jake raced down the trail, not daring to look behind him. The cougar was after the deer. But what if it didn't catch it? Would a couple of young kids start looking tasty?

They sped around curves and over dips and bumps. Lexie was going fast. Tommy had a hard time keeping up to her, and Jake soon passed him. Jake had never skied this fast before. The trees were a blur, and the wind stung his cheeks. He wanted to slow down, but the image of the cougar was still in his mind.

Jake crouched over his skis. Faster and faster he went, catching up to Lexie. They reached the bottom of the slope and kept going. He snowplowed into the curve, barely missing a tree as he swept around the bend.

They continued down the run. Lexie glanced back, and then so did Jake. Tommy was a little way behind them. He looked scared.

"Look out!" shouted Tommy.

Jake whipped his head around in time to see another sharp bend in the trail. He swerved and skidded around it. Lexie swerved too, but the run was narrow. Her skis caught on the soft deep snow at the edge of the run and she almost fell. Windmilling her arms, she headed straight toward a tree.

Jake heard a *THUNK*. It sounded like the crack of a baseball bat hitting a ball. He skidded to a stop. "Lexie!" he cried. He scrambled back up the slope.

Lexie was lying very still. Tommy snowplowed up beside Jake, got his skis crossed and tumbled forward.

"Lexie?" said Jake. He dropped to his knees and shook her gently. "Lexie? Are you all right?"

"What's wrong with her?" said Tommy. "Why won't she wake up?"

"She hit her head," said Jake.

"Is she—is she dead?" asked Tommy.

"No!" said Jake. "Don't be stupid." But Lexie hadn't moved, and she had a huge red mark on her forehead. Jake put his cheek close to Lexie's mouth,

just to check. He felt her breath, warm and moist on his skin. "She's just unconscious," he said.

"Un—un what?" said Tommy.

"Unconscious," Jake said. "Knocked out."

Lexie groaned. Her eyelids fluttered and then opened. "What happened?" she asked.

Jake was relieved to hear her speak.

"You missed the corner," said Tommy. "I yelled out to you, but Jake was in the way. So you ran into the tree."

Jake glared at Tommy. "That's not what happened," he said. "I didn't make Lexie run into the tree. The trail was too narrow, and she went off the run."

"But she could have made it around the corner, if you hadn't been there," said Tommy.

"And she would have seen it and slowed down in time if she hadn't been worrying about you," said Jake.

"It was an accident," said Lexie. "And I'm fine. It's just a bump. I've had worse." She tried to sit up, and then put a hand to her head. "I'm dizzy," she said.

Jake studied Lexie's face. She looked pale. She took her helmet off. Wisps of hair poked out all over her head. "Have you got your cell phone?" he asked.

Lexie nodded and rummaged in her pocket. Jake punched in 9-1-1.

"Hurry, Jake," said Tommy. "She doesn't look good."

Jake shook the phone and held it to his ear again. He frowned.

"What's wrong?" said Tommy.

"The phone's not working," said Jake. "The battery must be dead."

Chapter Five
EMERGENCY

Jake felt sick. Lexie was hurt. They had to get help. But they couldn't leave her on the ski hill alone.

"I'll be all right in a minute," said Lexie. She closed her eyes.

Jake wasn't so sure. "We should try to get you warm," he said.

"How? We're on the top of a mountain, remember?" said Lexie, not opening her eyes.

"Maybe Dad's got something in his backpack," said Tommy.

"Good idea," said Jake. He shrugged off the pack and started searching through it. "Here's a flashlight," he said, "and a first-aid kit, a Swiss Army knife, a candle and matches." He pulled Dad's cell phone out and switched it on. "This one's dead as well. We must be too far away from the lodge to get phone coverage." He tossed it back in the bag and pulled out a long slender object. It was red and white with a plastic cap on top. "A flare!"

"Hurray!" said Tommy.

"There are instructions on the side," said Jake. He squinted at the words. The light was fading fast. "Get the flashlight."

Tommy shone the light on the flare while Jake read carefully.

"Okay, I got it," Jake said. He took the cap off the top of the flare and stared at the hard black substance beneath. "It's like striking a match, I think."

Lexie opened her eyes and looked up at him. "Don't hold it too close to you," she said. "And get out in the open."

Jake moved toward the run and held the flare at arm's length.

"Be careful," said Tommy.

Jake took a deep breath. He fixed the cap onto his finger and positioned it on the igniter button. Pushing down, he flicked the scratchy surface of the cap across the igniter.

Bright light burst from the end of the flare. It spit and spluttered like a giant sparkler. Jake turned his eyes away.

"Whoa!" said Tommy. "That is so cool."

Jake stood holding the flare as far away from himself as possible. It was brighter than he had thought it would be. He could feel the heat, even through his glove.

Lexie struggled to a sitting position. "Aren't those things supposed to shoot up into the air?" she asked. "How is anyone supposed to see it?"

Jake frowned. Lexie was right. They were high on the mountain. It was almost dark, and the lodge was far away, on the other side of the hill. Jake didn't even know if enough time had passed for Dad to send out a search party. If no one was looking for them, the flare wouldn't do any good.

"You have to get it up above the trees," said Lexie. "Throw it."

Jake looked toward the treetops. They were awfully high.

"Throw it, Jake," said Tommy. "Quick, before it burns out."

Jake moved farther up the hill and climbed onto a big rock at the edge of the run. He needed to get as high as he could before he threw the flare.

I am a world-class javelin thrower, he thought. *This is my last chance for a world record. I must throw higher and farther than I have ever thrown before.*

He aimed for the top of the tallest tree he could see, swung his arm back and let it fly.

It was his best fielder's throw. If he had been on the baseball field, the flare would have made it to home plate, easy. But in the forest, throwing straight up, it barely made it to the top of the nearest tree.

Jake watched the flare light up the branches. The snow glowed bright orange-red. Then the flare fell back to the ground. The lighted end stuck in the snow, and the flare went out.

Chapter Six
SHELTER

Jake groaned.

"You didn't throw it high enough," said Tommy.

"Well, next time you do it," Jake said. He climbed down from the rock.

Tommy plucked up the dead flare and held it in the air. "Okay, I'll have a go. Light it again."

"You can't light it again, genius," said Jake. "Don't you know anything?"

Tommy looked hurt, which made Jake even more annoyed.

Lexie tried to stand and sat down again with a thump. She put her head in her hands. "Someone should go get help," she said. "I don't think I can ski."

Tommy shook his head. "Dad always says to stick together. We have to stay here with you."

"But—" said Lexie.

"No, Tommy's right," Jake said. "We should both stay here. Besides, it's almost dark. It would be too dangerous to ski down now. We'll have to wait for someone to come and find us."

"How long will that be?" asked Tommy.

"Not too long," said Jake. "They'll send out a search party once Mom and Dad report us missing. But we need to keep warm."

"We could light a fire," said Tommy.

"Where would we get dry firewood?" said Jake. "Everything's covered in snow." Then he remembered something he had seen in a documentary. "That's it," he said. "We build a snow fort. It keeps the cold air out, and the warm air in. That's why Dad had the candle in his pack. The candle warms up the air in the shelter." He grinned. "Let's get building."

Jake knew Lexie shouldn't move too much. She was sitting against a fallen tree, so they used the tree as the back wall of the snow fort and built the other walls around her. It was hard work. After they had used up the snow close by, they had to carry snow from farther away.

Jake had made lots of snow forts before. He hoped the roof wouldn't cave in, like it did at Lexie's last winter when they had a big snowball fight. All the kids in the neighborhood joined in, and just when Jake and Tommy finished restocking their fort, the roof caved in and they lost all their snowballs.

I am a master builder, thought Jake. *I am building the foundations for a great building. A pyramid, a cathedral, the Coliseum. This building will stand for centuries to come.*

"We have to reinforce the roof so it doesn't cave in," he said. He dug through Dad's pack until he found the Swiss Army knife. "I'll get some branches."

He stepped into the trees and shone the flashlight into the darkness above. Most of the lower branches were weak and spindly. The higher ones were too thick to cut with the knife. Jake moved farther into the forest. He couldn't hear Tommy anymore. The woods were quiet. The snow squeaked beneath his ski boots, and his breathing was harsh and ragged. He tried not to think about the cougar.

Jake stopped in front of a small bushy fir with slender branches along the lower part of its trunk. He propped the flashlight against the tree, grabbed a long feathery branch and sawed at it with his knife. The scent of fresh sap stung his nose. Before too long, the branch broke away. He hacked off five more and gathered them into his arms. As he turned to go back, he saw something move in the dark. He spun around, shining the light in that direction.

Nothing was there.

Jake hurried off, following his tracks back through the trees. It was hard to run in the deep snow.

He flashed the light around, hoping to scare off anything that might be watching him. Was the cougar still out there? he wondered.

Tommy and Lexie were huddled together, waiting for him.

"What took you so long?" asked Tommy. "We thought the cougar got you."

"Of course it didn't," said Jake. He glanced back into the trees. "I just wanted to find the right kind of branches."

Tommy helped Jake place the branches across the top of the shelter to make a roof. They carefully packed snow on top to seal the cracks. As they crawled through the opening, it started to snow.

It was dark inside the shelter, even darker than outside, and cold. Tommy huddled next to Lexie as Jake stuck the candle into the snow and lit it. A soft glow filled the shelter. The candle flame was small. Jake didn't know how it would keep them warm.

I am an Inuit fisherman, thought Jake. *I shelter from the storm in my igloo. It keeps me warm and snug through the night.*

It was very quiet inside the shelter. The falling snow smothered any noise from the forest. Jake knew they should try to stay awake. He remembered hearing you shouldn't let someone go to sleep if they had hit their head. Besides, if they all fell asleep, they wouldn't hear the search and rescue team. Jake told jokes and tried to get Lexie talking about school and the new computer she had been given for Christmas. But it had been a long exhausting day. Before long, Tommy and Lexie fell asleep.

Jake told himself he had to stay awake and keep watch. Each time his eyes closed, he pinched himself and rubbed his hands over his face to wake up. Finally he couldn't fight it any longer, and he drifted into a heavy slumber.

Chapter Seven
THE LAST RUN

When Jake woke, it was still dark, and the candle had burned almost halfway down. He was cold. Really cold. Jake took off his gloves and blew on his hands. His fingers were white and ghostly in the light from the candle.

Lexie and Tommy were curled up against the tree. Were they as cold as he was? he wondered. He knew it was dangerous to get too cold. They could get hypothermia. Jake nudged them with his foot.

"Lexie! Tommy!" he said. "Wake up."

Tommy sat up and rubbed his eyes. "Are we rescued?"

"No," said Jake. "You fell asleep. We all fell asleep. We have to stay awake, remember?"

"We're lucky the candle didn't go out," said Lexie.

Jake nodded. "How do you feel?" he asked.

Lexie pulled herself up and frowned. "My head hurts," she said. "But I'm not dizzy anymore." She turned her head from side to side to make sure. "Yeah, not great, but better. And I'm starving."

"Me too!" said Tommy. "Is there any food in Dad's bag?"

Jake searched the pockets of Dad's backpack and found two granola bars. He split one of them into three and gave everyone a piece.

"We should save the other one in case we need it later," he said.

Lexie shuffled over to the opening of the shelter.

"It's stopped snowing," she said. She crawled out, and Jake and Tommy followed.

The snow had stopped, and a full moon shone down through a break in the clouds. Jake stretched his tired muscles. He had thought it was cold in the shelter, but it was nothing compared to outside. If they hadn't built the shelter, they would have frozen.

"What are we going to do now?" asked Tommy. "I don't want to stay here anymore. I'm scared."

Jake didn't want to stay either. Even in the shelter it was freezing, and the woods were dark and spooky. Dad thought they had gone down Easy Street. No one would be looking for them on Wildcat Run. It could be hours before anyone found them.

He looked up at the sky. The clouds were clearing. The full moon lit up the trail like floodlights.

"Do you think you could make it to the lodge?" he asked Lexie.

Lexie hesitated. She glanced at Tommy and nodded. "Yeah, let's get out of here," she said.

Jake led the way down the hill. It had snowed a lot while they slept. It was hard skiing in the fresh powder. Their skis sunk into the snow, and it was

hard to turn. Tommy fell three times going around a steep curve. Lexie looked tired and weak.

Jake liked the feel of the powder. He liked making tracks in the new snow, and he liked the way it swirled around his skis as he shifted from side to side.

I am an alpine heli-skier, he thought. *The helicopter has dropped me at the top of a mountain. No one has ever skied these slopes before.*

He plowed around another bend, and that's when he saw it. The cougar.

Jake slid to a halt and raised his arms to stop Tommy and Lexie. He put a finger to his lips and pointed.

The cougar stood at the edge of a stream. The moon shone on its tawny coat. It was looking away from them, into the trees. Jake didn't think it had seen them. Not yet.

They watched as the cougar slowly lowered its head to drink. Jake thought he could hear it lapping the water, like his cat Ginger did at home.

The cougar raised its head. Jake held his breath. Could it smell them? Would it look around and see them? He kept as still as he could. The cat seemed in no hurry. It licked a paw and then put it down again. Its ears twitched, and for a moment Jake thought it could hear them. Then, without warning, the cougar leaped across the stream and disappeared into the trees.

Jake let out his breath.

"Did you see—?" Tommy started, but Jake shushed him.

"Let's go," Lexie mouthed.

Jake sped down the hill as fast as he dared. He kept one eye on Tommy and Lexie, and the other on the forest around them. The new powder, which he had enjoyed before, now seemed to catch at his skis and drag him down. The wind was icy cold on his cheeks.

They skied around bend after bend, down long slopes and through steep dips. They didn't slow down for anything. Finally they came to an open area, and Jake saw the ski lifts.

"Look!" he shouted. "There's the lodge."

Chapter Eight
RESCUE RIDE

Below them, a cluster of snow-covered buildings sat at the bottom of the hill. A group of people wearing bright orange jackets was gathered near the lifts.

"Over here!" Jake shouted, waving his arms.

Someone from the search party turned in their direction and started up the hill toward them.

"Mom! Dad!" Tommy cried.

Soon Jake, Lexie and Tommy were surrounded. The three of them were wrapped in silver-lined blankets, and a medic took Lexie aside to examine her head.

"We searched Easy Street and Gentle Giant three times," said Dad. "We even sent a team down

Lollipop Lane, although I couldn't imagine you going down there."

"No one remembered seeing you anywhere," said Mom.

Jake gulped.

"We went down Wildcat Run," said Tommy. "It was awesome. I went so fast, and then Lexie ran into a tree, and she was un-un—"

"Unconscious," Jake said. Dad's face was turning red. He always went red when he was angry.

"Yeah, unconscious," said Tommy. "And we built a shelter and used the candle from your bag to keep us warm."

"Did you say Wildcat Run?" asked a man who seemed to be in charge. The badge on his jacket said *Ed Lowrey*. "That run was closed late this afternoon. Someone said they spotted a cougar."

"It's true," said Tommy. "We saw it, didn't we, Jake?"

Jake nodded. "Twice," he said. "We were trying to get away from it when Lexie hit her head."

Dad frowned. "You should never have gone down Wildcat Run in the first place," he said.

"That was dangerous," said Mom.

"I know," said Jake. He couldn't look at his parents. "I'm sorry."

"Don't blame Jake," said Lexie, squeezing through the crowd of rescuers. "It was my idea."

"Thanks, Lexie," Jake said. "But I wanted to do it as much as you. I could have said no. I didn't think anything would happen."

"No one ever does," said Mom. She drew them into a group hug.

"We'll talk about it later," said Dad. "I'm just glad you are safe."

"And making a shelter," said Ed Lowrey, "that was good thinking, kids." He gestured toward the rescue sleds. "Now, how about a ride down to the lodge?"

"Hurray!" said Tommy. He jumped on the nearest sled with his skis still on. Dad laughed and unclipped them.

Jake and Lexie took off their skis and hopped on another sled. Jake was surprised at how tired he was. He was glad he didn't have to ski anymore. He was glad to be back, and he was glad he didn't have to be brave anymore.

Tommy turned around and tugged on his mom's coat. "Jake said we could have hot chocolate. Please?"

Mom laughed. "Yes, Tommy. You can have hot chocolate."

"With extra marshmallows?" Tommy said.

"With extra marshmallows," said Mom.

Jake grinned at Lexie. Maybe little brothers weren't such a pain after all.

Sonya Spreen Bates was born in the United States but moved to Victoria, British Columbia, when she was very young. She began writing children's fiction in 2001, inspired by her two daughters and their love of the stories she told them.

She is the author of *Marsh Island* and *Smuggler's Cave* (Orca Book Publishers). Her short stories have been published in school magazines in Australia and New Zealand. *Wildcat Run* is her third book with Orca. She currently lives in Adelaide, Australia.

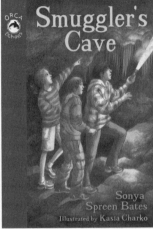